RACING BIKES

Jessica Kent

Edited by **Judy Tatchell**

Consultants: **Patrick Field**
and **Tricia Liggett**

Designed by **Richard Johnson**

Additional designs by **John Beaumont**

Cover design by **Stephen Wright**

Illustrated by **Kim Raymond**
and **Kuo Kang Chen**

Colour photography by **David Cannon, Allsport UK**
Black and white photography by **Jane Munro Photography**

Models: **Stuart** and **Rachel McGee, Colin Clarke**
and **Catherine Harthill**

This book was produced in association with

Contents

Using this book

To be a successful racing cyclist, you need a combination of good technique and tactical skill. This book can help you develop the style, strategies and mental approaches that will help you win different types of races.

In a road race, you have to conserve your energy so that you can make your main efforts at strategic moments. ▶

For some track races, you need to be a wily tactician. Others rely solely on speed and determination. ▶

You have to do without other riders spurring you on when you race against the clock in a time trial. ◀

You face many different situations and obstacles in cyclo-cross which require special techniques. ◀

Training

Consistent training is a must. This book tells you how to get yourself in condition by following a training program of exercise both on and off the bike.

Joining a club

Joining a local cycle club can benefit you, too. You get coaching and it is easier and more fun to train with other people. You need to belong to a club to enter most races.

Bike technology

There are certain design features unique to racing bikes. In this book, you can find out about bike technology and how performance can be improved.

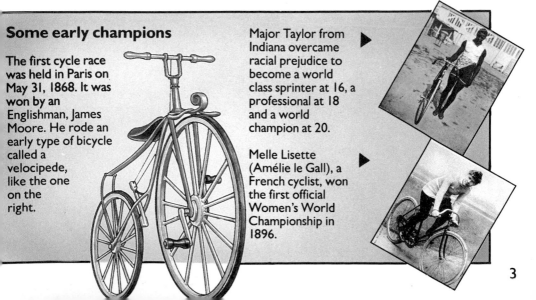

Some early champions

The first cycle race was held in Paris on May 31, 1868. It was won by an Englishman, James Moore. He rode an early type of bicycle called a velocipede, like the one on the right.

Major Taylor from Indiana overcame racial prejudice to become a world class sprinter at 16, a professional at 18 and a world champion at 20. ▶

Melle Lisette (Amélie le Gall), a French cyclist, won the first official Women's World Championship in 1896. ▶

About racing bikes

How fast a racing bike can go depends on its design and how light it is as well as on your skill as a rider.

Here are some of the special features of a standard racing bike.

Frame

Racing frames are made of lightweight alloy steel tubing. Professional machines may be made of aluminum or carbon fiber which are even lighter and much more expensive.

The forks are straighter than on an ordinary bike to make the steering more responsive. The chainstays are short, making the bike more rigid and efficient. These leave no room for mudguards.

Toeclips

Toeclips help you to exert pressure on the pedal all the way around: you can pull up as well as push down. An alternative design of pedal, called a system pedal, secures your shoe to the pedal. (There is more about these on page 42.)

Handlebars

Dropped handlebars let you to crouch low and keep a streamlined shape.

Saddle

A racing saddle is very narrow at the front. This reduces rubbing on the inside of your thighs.

Brakes

Racing bikes have side-pull brakes which allow you to brake slowly or hard.

As you brake, the cable is pulled up. This draws the arms (calipers) together and the rim is squeezed between the brake blocks.

Hubs

Racing hubs have quick-release levers so that you can change a wheel in seconds if you have a puncture.

Top tube

Head tube

Cable

Caliper

Brake shoe

Rear sprockets and derailleur (see opposite)

Down tube

Seat tube

Forks

Seat stay

Water bottle and cage for long rides.

Crank

Chainset (see opposite)

Chainstay

Quick-release lever

Wheels and tires

Narrow wheel rims and tires reduce contact with the road. This cuts down on friction between the tires and the road (called rolling resistance) so the bike can go faster. Good rims and hubs are made of light aluminum alloy.

High-pressure, or wired-on, tires have a removable inner tube. You repair a puncture by patching the inner tube.

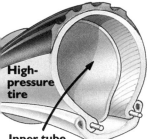

High-pressure tire

Inner tube

Tubular tires (tubs) have sewn-in tubes. The tire is glued on to the rim. Tubs are lighter than high-pressure tires but if you get a puncture they need repair by a specialist, making them expensive to use.

The alloy rims used with tubs are called sprints. You cannot use sprints with high-pressure tires.

Tubular tire

Sprint rim

Gears

Most racing bikes have ten or twelve gears. These help you to maintain an efficient pedaling rate, or cadence, on different surfaces and inclines.

Sprockets and chainwheels are described by the number of teeth they have. The set of five or six rear sprockets and freewheel mechanism is called a block.

Chain is shifted by derailleur and front changer (not shown).

A racing block might have sprockets with 13, 14, 15, 16, 17 and 18 teeth.

A racing chainset might have two chainwheels with 52 and 42 teeth.

How gears work

As you pedal, the distance the wheels travel is determined by the gear you are in. One turn of the pedals in a low gear will not take you as far as it will in a higher gear. A lower gear enables you to apply more pressure over a certain distance, for instance when you are going uphill or accelerating.

In the highest gear, the chain sits on the bigger chainwheel and the smallest sprocket.

Each time the pedals turn, the wheel goes around nearly four times.

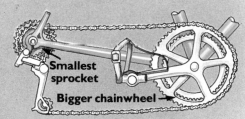

Smallest sprocket

Bigger chainwheel →

In the lowest gear, the chain sits on the smaller chainwheel and the biggest sprocket.

Each time the pedals turn, the wheel goes around just over twice.

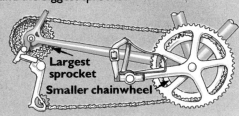

Largest sprocket

Smaller chainwheel

Getting started

You don't need a lot of specialist gear for cycle training but there are rules about what you can wear to enter some races. Also, certain items of clothing and equipment can make cycling more comfortable, efficient and safe. Some of these are shown below.

What to wear

The gear shown here is specially designed for cycling.* However, to start with you can wear shorts or a track suit for training, with a pair of athletics shoes.

Cycling shoes have stiff soles so that all your pedaling power is transmitted to the pedal. The force is distributed over the whole foot so your feet do not get so tired.

You can attach shoe-plates, or cleats, to the soles to keep the shoe in position on the pedal.

You should always protect your head with a helmet, whether training or racing. Helmets are often compulsory in races. You can find out more about different kinds of helmet on page 29.

Skin-tight shorts and shirts offer less wind-resistance than baggy clothes.

Cleat. Metal edge of pedal fits in groove.

Adjust the cleats so that your feet sit straight on the pedals. Otherwise you might damage your knees.

Walking around in cycling shoes reduces their stiffness and wears out the cleats so don't do it more than you have to.

Keeping warm

You get tired more quickly when you are cold. Thermal clothing is efficient but expensive. Instead, try wearing several thin, close-fitting layers under a cycling jersey. You can even put a few sheets of newspaper or a plastic bag up the front of your jersey to keep a cold wind off your chest.

Gloves

As well as being warm, gloves absorb vibrations from the road. They also protect your palms in a fall when your hands often hit the road first.

Be seen!

Bright clothes and fluorescent strips can save your life by warning motorists of your presence on the road.

*There is more about special clothing and equipment on pages 28-29 and 38-39.

Equipment and tools

You should be prepared to carry out minor repairs on any ride. Take a basic set of tools and equipment with you, such as the one shown on the right.

Put the tools in an old sock or roll them up in a rag and tie them under the saddle.

When you are out with a group, you only need one set of tools between you. Take your own spare inner tube, though.

Lights increase the chances of you being seen in the rain as well as in the dark.

Tire pump

Tire levers

Two inner tubes

Small screwdriver

Allen key

Puncture repair kit

Spare batteries

Spare bulbs

Lights

Small adjustable spanner

Setting up your bike

Check that your saddle and handlebars are adjusted to suit your height.* This helps you to use your leg, arm and back muscles efficiently as you ride.

Saddle height

Ask a friend to hold your bike. Sit with your hips level. With the crank at its lowest point and your foot flat on the pedal, your leg should be nearly straight.

With the cranks horizontal, your front knee should be directly over your toe. This is not easy to see for yourself so ask a friend to check for you. Move the saddle forward or back until it is right.

The top of the saddle should be horizontal.

There should be at least 5cm of the seat post inside the seat tube for safety.

Handlebars

You need to feel comfortable in these three positions.

▶ **On the drops: riding into the wind or sprinting.**

On the brake lever hoods: riding hard in a group or with a tail wind. ▶

◀ **On the tops: riding easily or when climbing in the saddle.**

To start with, set your bars about level with your saddle. As your back gets stronger, you can lower them for a more streamlined position. As a rough guide, the bars should prevent you from seeing the front hub when you are on the drops.

*You can find out how to make these adjustments on page 36.

Riding techniques

The techniques on this page are all quite basic but you need to be able to do them automatically and with confidence. Then you will be free to concentrate on the tactics which will help you win a race.

Ankling

Ankling technique increases the force you exert on the pedal. You use the toeclip to pull up as well as push down on it.

Pushing down.

Pulling up.

People develop different styles but the picture shows how your ankle might bend as you push down, pull back, pull up and push the pedal forward over the top.

Ankling is more effective at low cadences, for instance when you are climbing.

A cleat enables you to pull up and back on the pedal when your foot is pointing downward, without your foot slipping out of the toeclip.

Pedaling rate: cadence

In general, a fairly brisk cadence is the most efficient: you can keep a steady pressure on the pedals without getting too tired. When training, aim for a minimum average of between 75 and 100 pedal revolutions per minute, or rpm. (To find your rpm, count the revolutions in ten seconds and multiply by six.) Use your gears to maintain the cadence. Also, practice pedaling at a rate of 100 – 150 rpm for a few minutes at a time. This is good sprint practice.

Changing gear

To change gear smoothly without losing too much speed, keep pedaling but take the pressure off the pedals as you gently move the gear levers.

Limit your use of the inside chainwheel and the outside sprocket and vice versa. The steep angle of the chain slightly increases the friction between it and the chainwheel and sprocket.

If the chain comes off, ease off on the pedals. Try coaxing it back on by pedaling very lightly and gently moving the gear levers. You may be able to lean down and lift it back on to a chainwheel with your fingers. If these remedies do not work, don't risk jamming it: get off and replace it by hand.

Practice tip

Ankling with one leg at a time is very good practice. Take one foot out of its toeclip and make sure the other toestrap is tight.

Hold your free foot out of the way.

Try to keep an even pressure on the pedal

all the way around. Then change legs.

Reaching speed

Don't start in too low a gear or you will waste energy pedaling furiously and not getting very far. Try starting on the big chainwheel, one or two sprockets below the one you use for cruising. Or start on your cruising sprocket but on the little wheel. Then you just need to shift to the big one when your cadence has increased.

Climbing

Change down just before you reach a hill. If you leave it until half way up, you lose speed and may stall completely on a steep hill.

Stay in the saddle in your lowest gear for as long as you can. If you need more power, stand up on the pedals and use your weight to push down. This is called honking. Keep your weight back so that your back wheel does not slip.

Braking

★ Try to look ahead and avoid problems by slowing down gently rather than braking suddenly and losing more speed than necessary.

★ If you have to brake suddenly when riding fast, put both brakes on hard and then ease off the pressure as the bike slows down, to avoid skidding.

★ Use both brakes evenly. Too much pressure on the front brake may make the back wheel lift off. Braking too hard with the back brake can make the wheel skid.

★ Shift your body weight back and down as you brake to help stabilize the bike.

★ In the wet, your brakes may lose their grip on the slippery wheel rims. Brake rapidly on and off to clear water off of them so the brakes can grip properly.

Cornering at speed

If you must brake to get around a corner, do so as you approach it and not as you go round. Change down in advance so that you can accelerate out of the corner. Keep your weight back for stability.

The faster you go, the more you lean into the corner. Stop pedaling and make sure your inside pedal is up or it might catch the ground and you will fall off.

On sharp corners, hold your inside knee away from your body to act as a counter-weight.

You corner faster at the front in a race. Near the back, you have to brake earlier as the leaders slow down for the bend. By the time you reach it, they are speeding off ahead, leaving a gap for you to close.

To keep your speed up, try to smooth the bend off by swinging out slightly as you enter it. Look behind before you do this and NEVER cross into the opposite lane.

Bike-handling

The faster you go on your bike, the quicker your reactions need to be. You have to be able to take immediate avoiding action when suddenly confronted with a deep pothole, a car door opening in your path or even a fallen cyclist. The following techniques can help you tackle such hazards.

Practice these techniques where there are no other vehicles and where you will have a soft landing if you fall.

Avoiding obstacles

Here is a quick way to whip around an obstacle in your path while barely losing speed. To start with, don't practice with an obstacle that might damage you or your bike if you crash.

Reduce speed very slightly as you approach the obstacle.

Just before you reach it, flick your handlebars towards it. This makes the bike lean away from the obstacle.

As the bike leans away from the obstacle, steer away from it. The lean helps you to make a very sharp turn around it.

Correct your course to continue.

Jumping the bike

If you don't have room to steer around an obstacle or pothole, you may need to jump over it. Practice this without an obstacle first. Then try jumping something low that will not damage the wheels if you land on it.

Accelerate hard. Then freewheel for a moment as you throw your weight back and pull up on the handlebars to lift the front wheel.

As soon as the front wheel comes up, throw your weight forward and pull up on the pedals using your toeclips. This lifts the back wheel.

You will find that the faster you are traveling, the further you can jump on the bike.

Practice lifting the back wheel before the front wheel touches the ground. Then see if you can do the whole jump in one movement: lift your body sharply, then bend your arms and legs to bring the bike up with you.

Jumping sideways

You can combine the previous two techniques to jump across a ridge or a rut in a road or track. Try practicing with a chalk line to represent a ridge.

Steer sharply away from the ridge to make the bike lean toward it. As soon as this happens, steer toward it.

As you steer toward the ridge, pull up sharply on the handlebars to lift the front wheel up over it.

As the front wheel lifts off the ground, lean forward and pull up on the toeclips to lift the back wheel.

As you get better at doing this, you should find that you can lift both wheels off the ground at the same time.

Dips and potholes

Crashing through dips and potholes puts strain on both you and your bike. Shift your weight as shown to reduce this.

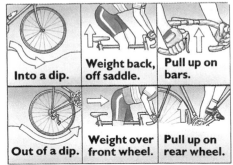

| Into a dip. | Weight back, off saddle. | Pull up on bars. |
| Out of a dip. | Weight over front wheel. | Pull up on rear wheel. |

Rough roads

On bumpy surfaces, keep your weight just off the saddle and bend your arms a bit. Your bent limbs act as shock absorbers.

Supporting your weight on the pedals keeps the center of gravity low. It may be easier to use a higher gear than normal.

Practice tips

★ Don't practice the jumping and avoidance techniques on the open road until you are sure you have mastered them.

★ Wear a thick tracksuit, gloves and a helmet to protect yourself.

★ If you fall, protect your head by folding your arms around it. You can find out more about falling on page 41.

★ Try to stay relaxed even in awkward situations. If you tense up, you will ride erratically.

11

Time trials

A time trial is a flat-out race against the clock over a fixed distance. Most take place on the open road but there are also time trials on cycle tracks. Because they are timed, they can help you to measure your own improvement.

Time trials for under-16s are usually between 10 and 40km long. Senior races can be up to 160km. Competitors start at one-minute intervals and follow a marked route, with marshals to direct you at road junctions.

Before the race

Time trials are extremely demanding so you need to warm your muscles up before you start. (In general, the shorter an event, the longer the warm up, because the start will be more violent.) A good way to warm up is to ride to the start if it is not more than an hour's gentle ride away. Then do some stretches such as those on pages 24-25.

Practice tip

At the start of a race you need a helper to hold your bike up as shown. Ask someone to practice this with you. They can either hold the lip of the saddle at the back or stand next to you, holding the seat post and handlebars.

Start with the cranks about 11 o'clock and 5 o'clock. Try to get a powerful start with no wobbling.

The time trial bike

You can ride a time trial on any racing bike but keep it as light as you can. If you can afford them, you can buy special time trial wheels which have fewer spokes to cut down on weight.

As most courses are fairly flat, you can remove a chainwheel: five or six close-ratio gears* are enough. The block should allow you to keep your feet spinning at 100rpm at least.

*Each sprocket on a close-ratio block has one more tooth than the last. This gives you a lot of choice within a fairly small range.

During the race

Keep your focus on the road ahead. Don't look back or you will lose concentration and speed.

Maintain a steady cadence throughout. Counting your pedal revolutions can help you strike up a rhythm.

Maintain your effort just below the point at which you become exhausted. If you go over this limit, you will waste time slowing down to recover.

Race tip

As you don't have many gears, you may have to rise out of the saddle to keep your cadence up on hills.

Technique tip

Keep your body low, your elbows tucked in and your head still for minimum aerodynamic drag.

Team time trials

In a team time trial, teams of two or four riders compete over a course of up to 100km. Members of the team take turns at the front to keep the pace up.* The time registered is that of the second person of a team of two or the third of a team of four.

Race food

In an event of 40km or more, you will need water. Over 75km you will also need food or an energy drink to keep up your energy reserves.**

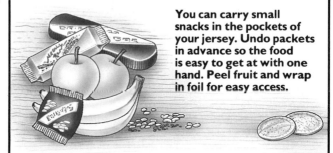

You can carry small snacks in the pockets of your jersey. Undo packets in advance so the food is easy to get at with one hand. Peel fruit and wrap in foil for easy access.

Start drinking after about 15 minutes. Don't wait until you are thirsty. Eating and drinking little and often saves your body from having to work hard at digestion.

Eat or drink when you are riding on the flat and in a straight line: climbing, descending and cornering demand your full concentration.

Water is heavy, so experiment on training runs to find out how much you need. Don't forget you will need more on hot days.

*See page 15 for more about riding in a group.
**See page 43 for more about food and energy drinks.

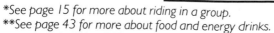

Road racing

In a road race, you race against other riders, not the clock. This calls for different tactics.

Most road races are massed start events, where all the riders start together. These are called scratch races. In others, called handicap races, some categories of entrant such as Juniors (see right) may be given a head start.

(see right)

Closed-circuit races

Some races are held on routes closed to traffic on town centers, parks or, industrial estates. These are called criteriums. All Juvenile races are held on closed circuits because Juveniles are not allowed to race on the open road.

In a race on the open road, a car with a warning sign travels in front and marshals stand along the route. You have to obey all the rules of the road.

Race distances

Juvenile races are usually 16 or 40km long. Junior races vary between 40 and 100km. More senior races are usually 100-120km but may be up to 200km long.

You score points for doing well in a race and move up a category when you have scored the necessary number of points.

Before the race

Before the race, your bike will be checked by officials to make sure it is roadworthy.

Try to position yourself somewhere near the front in a massed start to avoid being delayed by slow starters. This is particularly important in criteriums which tend to start very fast.

Categories

Professionals . . paid team members
Firsts . . . . . . top class amateurs
Seconds . . second class amateurs
Thirds . . . . other riders over
Juniors . . . . 16-18 year o[l]
Juveniles . . . . under
Veterans . . . . over

Practice tip

Practice pushing off and getting your free foot into the toeclip before the crank has completed one revolution. This is better than trying to get your foot in and speed up at the same time.

Riding in a bunch

By tucking in close behind another rider, you can travel as fast as him or her with 15-20% less effort. This is called slipstreaming or wheel-following. A group, or bunch, can travel faster for longer than a lone rider by taking turns at the front. This is called doing bit and bit.

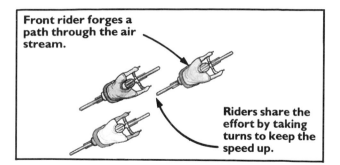

Front rider forges a path through the air stream.

Riders share the effort by taking turns to keep the speed up.

During the race

During the race, the field splits up as smaller groups make an effort to pull away from the main group. This is called making a break or attacking.

Tactics for road racing involve riding with a bunch and co-operating by taking turns at the front. In this way the bunch can travel fast while conserving energy.*

Toward the end of a race you need to be in a bunch near the front. There may be a sprint finish between you and the other members of the group. If you have enough energy left, you may be able to make a lone break at the end and leave the others behind.

Take care – if your wheel touches the wheel of the rider in front, you will go over the handlebars.

If there is a sidewind, take shelter accordingly. You can find out more about this over the page.

WIND

Race tips

★ Keep your turns at the front short. Make sure everyone shares the work.
★ Stay alert: look past the rider in front so that you can spot hazards ahead.

Practice tip

Wheel-following requires concentration and a very steady speed. Practice by leaving a bike's length between you and the bike in front. As you get used to riding at an even pace, you can gradually reduce this to a minimum of 15cm.

*There is more about this and other race tactics on the next two pages.

Road race tactics

It often takes more than power and speed to win. Road race tactics are all about saving energy, placing yourself in the bunch correctly, bluffing and knowing when to relax or make a break. You learn from experience so enter races even if you don't have much chance of winning. Use them to observe and experiment with different tactics.

Before a race

If possible, ride the course before the race or study it on a good map. Note the difficult sections such as hills, corners, narrow or winding sections or areas exposed to the wind. These can be good places to make breaks because the general pace tends to slow down. You need to be near the front on these sections so that you can join any breaks that form.

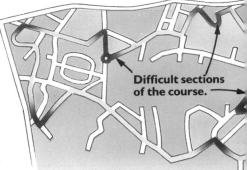

Difficult sections of the course.

Taking shelter

If there is a side wind in a road race, move to the sheltered side of the rider in front. If the road is closed to traffic, the whole bunch can string out across it as shown on the left. This shape is called an *echelon*. If there is traffic on the road, it is not safe to form groups of more than three riders.

You share the effort by taking turns leading. As a rough guide, turns might last from about 100m to about 500m, depending on the effort needed to keep the pace up. In a small group, you need to take longer turns.

Going downhill, a bunch tends to string out for safety and then regroup at the bottom. Going uphill, try to maintain your cadence rather than your speed.

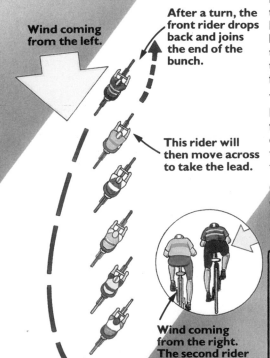

Wind coming from the left.

After a turn, the front rider drops back and joins the end of the bunch.

This rider will then move across to take the lead.

Wind coming from the right. The second rider shelters on the left.

Changing leaders

After a turn at the front, glance back to check that the road is clear behind you and to let the other riders know you are about to drop back.

Keep close in as you move back. Accelerate in time to join the back of the bunch or you may drop off the end.

Attacking

In a race, you need to balance energy conservation with riding hard to gain a lead. As you begin an attack, ride hard for about 500m without looking back. Then glance around to see if you have broken away and which riders have followed you.

A bunch is sometimes called a *peloton* (pronounced "pellaton"). This is the French word for it.

In the break

In a break a long way from the finish, it is important to work together to keep the pace up. Only try to split the group up when you feel you have a good chance of getting to the finish alone.

If you need to engage a higher gear to lead a break, do it before you hit the front so that you can concentrate on maintaining your speed.

If you want to overtake, ride up on the sheltered side of the group.

Don't attempt to join every break or you will get exhausted. Choose your moments, such as the following:

★ Where other riders are slowing down in difficult sections of the race.
★ Join breaks led by strong riders. These are more likely to succeed.

If you cannot keep up with a break, don't waste energy trying to catch up. Sit up, change down, have a drink, ride steadily and rejoin the bunch.

Race tip

Don't attack from the front where your intentions are obvious to everyone. Go from further down the bunch where you can shoot by and surprise the leaders.

Bluffing

If you are feeling the strain of a race, it is likely that others are too. Appearing in control will dishearten them. Ride confidently and try to hide your discomfort. If you then try to attack, they may let you go, thinking your are too strong for them.

Mental preparation

A race is a personal thing. Some riders feel they must calm themselves before an event while others need to wind themselves up. Don't worry if you cannot sleep the night before a big race. A good night's rest two nights before does you as much good.

Preparing for pain

Push yourself during your training so that you can identify the difference between pain you can ignore and pain that warns of injury. Try not to be put off by physical pain early in a race. Breathe deeply and hang on. Things should soon get easier.

Track racing

Track racing is the fastest form of cycle racing. Both the bikes and the track itself are designed for maximum speed. The ends of the track are steeply banked to help you corner at top speed and the smooth surface cuts down on rolling resistance. Tracks may be indoors or outdoors, with wooden, asphalt or concrete surfaces.

Using the banking

The banked ends of the track help you to stay close to the center and keep your speed up without slipping as you corner.

You can also use the bank cunningly in races which require tactics as well as speed. It can give you acceleration so that you can swoop down to overtake or intimidate an opponent. Or you can "block" them against the barrier at the top and speed off down the bank in front.

Riding a track bike

A track bike has neither brakes nor gears. There is no freewheel mechanism so you cannot stop pedaling while the bike is in motion. You slow down by restraint on the pedals. This takes some time to get used to, so be careful.

The track

200m line

Sprinter's line

Finish line

Gauge line

Stayer's line

Pursuit start and finish lines.

The lines are used in the races described opposite.

The Olympic standard length for a cycle track is 333.3m but track lengths can vary. A track is measured along the bottom line, or gauge line. You are not allowed to ride below this line.

Race tip

The shortest route around the track follows the gauge line. Riding close to this will help you to lap the track quickly.

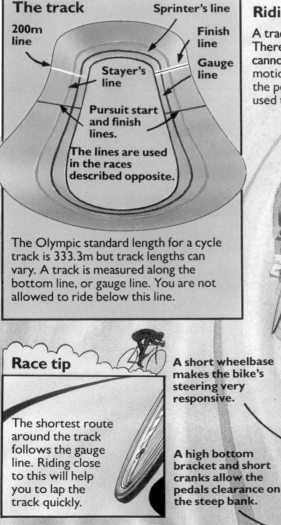

A bike with no freewheel is called a fixed wheel bike. Lack of brakes or gearing keeps the weight down.

A short wheelbase makes the bike's steering very responsive.

A high bottom bracket and short cranks allow the pedals clearance on the steep bank.

Having a go

Cycle clubs run "try-out" sessions on tracks. They will lend you a bike and give you some coaching. Later on, you can join the track league and take part in the races described below. Remember that track racing is fast and can be dangerous so don't be too ambitious.

Sprint races

In a sprint race, only the last 200m are timed. During the preceding laps, the two riders encourage each other to take the lead so that they can slipstream behind, saving energy for the final sprint.

Tactics are based on bluff and agility. If you are in front, you can try to make your opponent overtake by accelerating and then suddenly slowing down. You can even balance motionless on the track (see below). However, time your tactics carefully so that you are in a position to lead the last 200m.

Track League			
NAME	CLUB	RACE POINTS	RUN TOTAL
T. Ross	Bathby C.C.	6	35
A. Smith	Elmouth C.C.	8	42
S. Leach	Leyton Club	12	28

Practice tip

To practice balancing motionless on the track keep both pedals horizontal and rock them slightly. Try it where the banking begins at the end of the straight. Turn your handlebars into the bank to help you balance.

Devil take the hindmost

In these races, usually called "devils", the last rider over the line at the end of each lap is withdrawn until only two or three are left. These riders then sprint around the last lap. It is illegal to overtake on the inside of a rider who is inside or on the sprinter's line.

Points races

In a points race, riders compete over a set distance. At the start of some laps, a whistle blows to indicate that these are sprint laps. Points are scored for these by the first three riders to complete them. Double points are scored for the last lap.

Pursuits

In a pursuit race, two riders compete aganst the clock and each other. They start at opposite sides of the track and try to catch up to each other. The rider who closes the gap wins the race. Otherwise the full length course is ridden and whoever covers it in the shortest time is the winner.

Madisons

A Madison is a points race in which up to 20 teams of two people race over a set distance. They take turns racing for a lap each. The person not racing rolls gently around the banking above the stayer's line (see previous page). At the changeover, they are pushed into the race by their partner. Only one rider sprints to the finish line.

To change places, you can use a technique called a handsling. First, you link hands.

Then throw your partner forward into the race and move back above the stayer's line.

Cyclo-cross

Cyclo-cross presents a different set of challenges from other kinds of cycle races. It combines cycling with running and carrying your bike, across rough ground and up and down steep hills. You usually get very muddy and wet. You need stamina and agility.

The cyclo-cross season runs through autumn and winter.

The race

Although you may fall off, you shouldn't get hurt since the race is off-road and the speed tends to be quite slow, with the riders strung out. After a massed start, you have to do as many laps as you can within a set time. Each lap is two or three kilometres long.

The bike and clothing

You can adapt a road bike by changing the gearing and fitting knobby tires but a true cyclo-cross bike has a few other differences, as shown below. Most races also allow mountain bikes.

The saddle should be about 5cm lower than on a road bike, for better control.

You can put shoulder pads into your jersey to help you support the bike.

Knobby tires grip in the mud.

Wear boots with studded heels for grip and support.

Handlebar gear levers let you change gear without taking your hands off the handlebars.

Cantilever brakes are more powerful than side-pull brakes. They also give more clearance between the brake arms and the wheels so they get less clogged with mud.

A high bottom bracket gives good ground clearance. A long wheelbase gives the bike more stability.

Gearing that gives you plenty of choice, such as a 13/28 block and 44 chainwheel, helps you to cope with different surfaces and inclines. You do not need gears as high as for road races.

Remove anything you don't need from the frame, such as a bottle cage or pump pegs, which may hurt you if you fall off.

Checking the course

★ Arrive early to give yourself time to ride the course before the event.

★ Look out for alternatives to the main path such as routes that avoid really muddy, churned-up ground.

★ Identify the firm ground on steep climbs.

★ Check out obstacles such as tree roots and drainage channels.

Descending

You are likely to encounter steep hills on cyclo-cross courses. You can tackle hills which appear almost vertical from above using the following technique. Practice on short, obstacle-free hills to start with.

Keep your weight back and just off the saddle with your arms almost straight and your pedals level.

Control your speed with the back brake only.

Gates and tree trunks

It is quickest to climb gates and fallen tree trunks with the bike on your shoulder. As you get used to this, you may even be able to vault them. Otherwise, swing your bike over and follow unladen.

Getting on and off

You need to be able to get on and off the bike quickly so that you can run with it. Loosen your toeclips so that you can slide your feet out easily.

As you prepare to get off, move your left foot back in the toeclip to help you remove it later. Take your right foot out of the clip.

Press down on the right-hand side of the bars and swing your right leg back over the saddle.

Bring your right leg between your left leg and the frame. Whip your left foot out of the clip and land on your right foot.*

Grab the down tube with your right hand and lift the bike on to your right shoulder.

Loop your right arm around the frame and grasp the lower rung of the left handlebar.

To remount, swing your right leg over the saddle. Don't touch the pedals until your bottom is on the saddle. Then flip the clips over and slide your feet in.

Race tip

Where you can, stay on the bike. It is usually faster to ride than to run with the bike.

Practice tip

Practice dismounting, running and remounting on level ground until you can do it smoothly without losing momentum. You could devise a circuit with trees and so on marking where you get on and off.

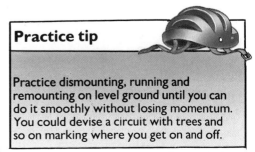

*If you are nervous about not getting your foot out in time, bring your right foot around the outside of your left leg instead.

Other cycling events

Other events with something a bit different to offer include cycle speedway, triathlons and hill climbs.

You can find the addresses of the organizations which arrange these races on page 45.

Cycle speedway

Cycle speedway is a fast and furious race that takes place on circuits normally between 50-100m long. The race is usually four laps and lasts about 45 seconds. Four riders compete at a time, either as individuals or as two teams of two.

Speedway technique

The bike has no brakes or gears, so you have to use your feet to slow down on corners.

You need to make a very fast start and aim to lead into the first corner. The skill lies in protecting your lead on subsequent corners.

To prevent a rider from sneaking by on the inside, you must stick close to the inside of the track. However, if as a result you swing out as you exit from a corner, an opponent could slip through.

Crash helmets are compulsory for training and racing on the track.

Lightweight frame

Nylon pedals with no grips or clips to scratch you in a fall.

Knobby tires

Clothing

You need to wear tough, clothing and thick gloves to protect you if you fall off. Strong boots or athletics shoes withstand the rough treatment they receive on corners and protect your feet.

Your body and energy

Different races make different energy demands on you. Your body mainly uses two systems to convert the food you eat into energy.

The aerobic system needs oxygen to provide a slow release of energy over a long period of time, such as during some stretches of a road race.

The anaerobic system mainly uses stored muscle glycogen. This provides a quick burst of energy for a short period, for instance during a sprint.

Most races demand a combination of both kinds of energy. Proper training stimulates the two energy systems.*

See pages 24-27 for information about training.

Triathlons and biathlons

A triathlon consists of three different sports: cycling, swimming and running. The course includes all three in continuous sequence. Course lengths vary but the following are recognized standards.

> **Olympic/International standard: swim 1500m, cycle 40km, run 10km.**
>
> **Mini triathlon: swim 500m, cycle 20km, run 5km.**

The season runs through spring and summer. You can save money on entry fees if you are a member of the national triathlon association.

A biathlon (or "run: bike: run" event) might involve 5km running, 30km cycling and another 5km running.

Hill climbs

Hill climbs are short but very grueling. Races may only last about five minutes but even so, some riders do not make it to the finish. You need to build up your levels of strength over many months of hard training.

It is better to start steadily and finish fast than to go off like a bullet and then collapse half way up. On a hill climb there is no respite from the incline where you can recover from oxygen debt (see below).

Experiment to find your most powerful position. It is likely to be up out of the saddle, using your arms and upper body to pull on the handlebars. Most people stand nearly all the way up, only sitting down on the lesser inclines for a few brief moments.

Riders start at intervals and race against the clock.

Relax your shoulders and keep your back flat. Hunching up will limit your oxygen intake.

When you stand for more power, grip the brake lever hoods and pull on them.

Hill climbs normally take place towards the end of the summer. They are organized by the national time trials association (see page 45).

Training

Strengthening the heart and lungs increases the amount of oxygen you can take in for aerobic energy production. Interval training (see page 27) helps to improve anaerobic energy production.

Oxygen debt

If you ride up a hill as fast as possible, after a while your legs start to ache unbearably and you gasp uncontrollably. This is because your body cannot take in enough oxygen to remove toxic waste from anaerobic energy production. This condition is known as oxygen debt.

If you slow down or stop, the toxic waste is removed in the bloodstream and your muscles will recover.

Basic fitness

The stronger your heart and lungs are, the more oxygen they can supply to your muscles and the longer you will be able to keep going in a race.

You also need plenty of power which comes from muscular strength and flexibility. The next four pages give you some ideas for how to develop all these aspects of fitness.

Stretching exercises

Gentle stretching helps to make you more supple. It also prepares the body for more strenuous activity and speeds up recovery afterwards. Here are some stretches which you can use as a warm-up before a training run or race.

Points to note

* Make sure you are warm before you start.

* Move slowly and relax into the positions – don't "bounce".

* Stretch carefully. It is not meant to hurt.

* Hold stretches for at least ten seconds.

* Try to stretch daily and after cycling as well as before.

Back of neck stretch

Stand up straight and clasp your hands round the back of your neck. Slowly drop your head forward bringing your elbows in and bending your knees slightly.

Side stretch

Stand with your feet apart and knees slightly bent. Support your body with your right hand on your hip. Stretch your left arm up and over to the side. Repeat other side.

Thigh stretch

Lie on your left side, supporting your head with your hand. Bend your right leg up and grip your ankle. Ease your leg back and hip forward, keeping your knees together. Repeat other side.

Lower back stretch

Lie on your back and pull both knees into your chest. Hold behind your knees.

Hamstring stretch

From the position above, place both hands behind your left thigh. Lower the other foot to the floor. Straighten your left leg until you feel a slight tension at the back of the leg. Hold the position, then repeat other side.

Calf stretch

Stand up straight and rest your hands against a wall. Step back with your left foot and straighten the leg, bending the right leg slightly. Keep your toes facing forwards. Change legs.

Chest and arm stretch

Kneel with your thighs vertical. Slide your hands along the ground until your nose nearly touches it. Press your shoulders towards the ground and try not to arch your back.

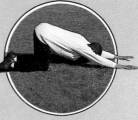

Building stamina

When cycling is not practical or you want some variety, running and swimming are good alternatives. You have to do an aerobic activity steadily for at least 20 minutes, three times a week, before it is effective in building stamina.

Building strength

Cycling uses the quadriceps muscle (at the front of your thigh) and the gluteal group (your buttocks). These must be strong but you also need strength in your upper body. Regular circuit and weight training can help to develop both stamina and strength. Find out about sessions at a sports center.

Circuit training

Circuit training consists of a series of exercises set up at different stations around a sports hall. Each presents a different task which you perform a number of times. You move from station to station until you have completed the circuit.

Weight training

Weight training should be supervised by a qualified coach. You start with light weights and progress to heavier ones. You need to be given a program which suits your age and fitness level.

Muscles and how they work

Muscles are made up of many thousands of fibers that can lengthen or shorten depending on the demand placed on them. A muscle contains a mixture of red and white fibers.

Red or slow-twitch fibers work when the demand is slower for longer distance riding. This is aerobic work.

Muscle fibers

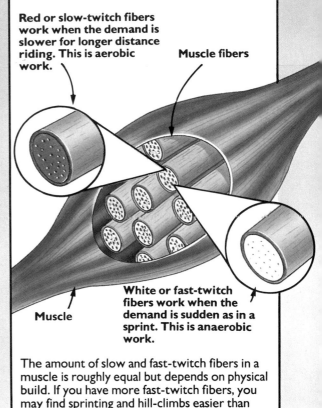

White or fast-twitch fibers work when the demand is sudden as in a sprint. This is anaerobic work.

Muscle

The amount of slow and fast-twitch fibers in a muscle is roughly equal but depends on physical build. If you have more fast-twitch fibers, you may find sprinting and hill-climbs easier than someone with more slow-twitch fibers. They may be able to keep going longer.

Training on the bike

You are far more likely to achieve sucess in racing if you put some thought into planning a proper training program. It is a good idea to record details of your training in a diary. Then when you hit winning form, you can look back to remind yourself how you achieved it.

Warming up

Warming up before a training ride will help your body to benefit. Do a few shoulder rotations and knee lifts followed by some stretches*. Then ride briskly for about 15 minutes before extreme exertion such as sprinting.

Keeping a training diary

Start by testing yourself over about ten kilometres. After warming up, take your pulse (see right) and begin your ride. Record the details shown below in your training diary. You can find out how you are improving by testing yourself over the same distance once a month.

Record similar details about all your training rides and also about the other activities included in your program.

Training diary
Pulse rate before:
after:
Date:
Time:
Distance:
Weather conditions:
Remarks: (Note how you felt during the ride and how long it took you to recover.)

Pulse rate

When you exert yourself, your muscles need more blood so your heart beats faster. Exercise strengthens your heart so that it pumps out the same amount of blood with fewer beats. This reduces your pulse rate.

Testing your pulse

You need a clock or watch with a second hand.

Rest your middle fingers on the inside of your wrist. You should feel a gentle throbbing.

Count how many beats you feel in ten seconds. Multiply this by six. This is your pulse rate per minute.

Finding your training zone

To exercise your heart muscles, you need to raise your pulse to within a training zone. This zone is 65% – 85% of your maximum recommended heart rate during exercise, or MHR. Find your MHR by subtracting your age from 220. This example shows how a 16-year-old would work out his or her training zone.

MHR during exercise: $220 - 16 = 204$

$$\frac{65}{100} \times 204 = 132 \quad \text{(lower end of zone)}$$

$$\frac{85}{100} \times 204 = 173 \quad \text{(upper end of zone)}$$

A 16-year-old's training zone is between 132 and 173 beats per minute. You need to work within your training zone for at least 20 minutes three times a week. Take your pulse immediately after a ride to see if you have been doing so.

Planning a training program

Below is an outline training program. It shows when different types of exercise are the most useful. How far you should ride and how often depends on your age and fitness, so seek advice from your club coach. In the race season, you can aim to be training or racing six days a week, with one day's rest.

	Preparation		Pre-race	Racing season		
	AUTUMN	WINTER	SPRING	SUMMER		
Stretching exercises	▬▬▬▬▬▬▬▬▬▬▬▬▬▬▬▬					Every day.
Circuit training	▬▬▬▬▬▬▬▬					Leave at least two days between each circuit or weight training session.
Running or swimming	▬▬▬▬▬▬▬▬					
Weight training						
Cycle training	▬		▬▬▬▬▬▬▬▬▬▬▬			Build stamina by high winter mileages. Then work on speed in the spring.
Racing	▬▬ Cyclo-cross ▬▬▬▬		▬▬▬▬▬▬▬			
Monthly mileage	100 80			150 200		

Training on the track

One method of sprint training is to ride 100m fast then 100m slow. This is called interval training. For long distance races, you can increase the distances of speed and recovery to one lap each. Don't exceed six sets per session.

Time trial training

Ride distances of 10-25km (up to 50km as you get fitter) at a steady, fast speed.

Road race training

Steady-state riding (riding at a little harder than an easy pace) and sprinting are good training. Aim to go out twice during the week for between half and one and a half hours, with a longer ride of three or four hours at the weekend.

Group training

Training with other people is more fun and you may find you can achieve more with others to urge you on or compete with. You can practise tactics such as wheel-following and attacking.

Warming down

If you stop exercising suddenly, you may feel faint or get stiff the next day. A warming down session will prevent this. Ride gently for the last 10-15 minutes and then repeat the stretches you did to warm up.*

*See pages 24-25.

27

Cycling kit

The cycling kit shown on this page is specially designed for efficiency, safety, comfort or visibility. You could start with the basics as shown on page 6 and build up your kit as you go along.

Race clothing

For most races, you wear skin-tight cycling jerseys and shorts. There may be rules about the colors you are allowed to wear. An all-in-one skinsuit is an alternative for short races where you don't need pockets to carry food.

Training in the cold

In cold weather, cycling can be a very chilly activity because of the rate at which you move through the air. The effect is similar to standing in a cold wind.

Concentrate on keeping your head and upper body warm. A padded, nylon-fronted jacket will help to keep the wind off.

Your legs tend to stay warmer because they are moving, so a pair of leggings (or tracksuit bottoms tucked into your socks) should be enough.

A racing cape is a type of waterproof jacket. Most are brightly colored to show up in the rain.

Extra clothes might slow you down a bit but this does not matter for training.

Wear white cotton socks for visibility. Tennis socks with a thick sole and heel are ideal.

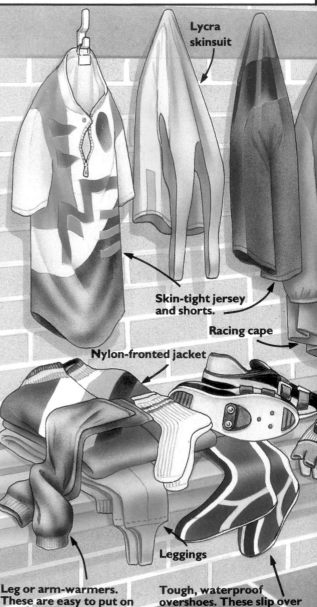

Lycra skinsuit

Skin-tight jersey and shorts.

Racing cape

Nylon-fronted jacket

Leggings

Leg or arm-warmers. These are easy to put on or take off if the weather keeps changing.

Tough, waterproof overshoes. These slip over your cycling shoes and have holes for the cleats.

Clothing accessories

Cycling glasses protect your eyes from dust and grit in the air. Some have lenses which block out harmful ultra-violet light.

A cap shades your eyes – or you can turn it around to shade the back of your neck. It absorbs sweat and you can wear one under a helmet. On its own, though, a cap won't protect you if you fall, so you should only wear one for easy riding on traffic-free roads.

Helmets

When buying a helmet, try it on, tighten the straps and shake your head to make sure it does not slip about on your head. Remember that a helmet will not be effective unless it is securely fastened. There are three main types of helmet to choose from, as shown below.

Cycling cap

Cycling glasses

Bike accessories

Cycling water bottles are easy to drink from. The bottle cage attaches to the down tube with metal clips or bottle eyes.

You cannot rely on testing bike light batteries by turning them on since even a dead one might give a short power surge. It is not easy to remember when you last replaced them so carry spares and bulbs.

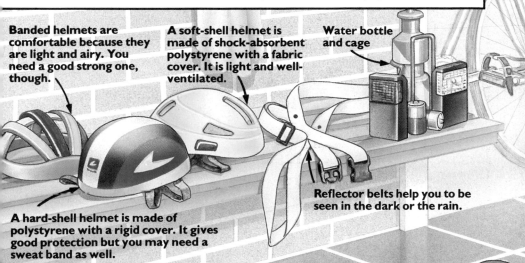

Banded helmets are comfortable because they are light and airy. You need a good strong one, though.

A soft-shell helmet is made of shock-absorbent polystyrene with a fabric cover. It is light and well-ventilated.

Water bottle and cage

A hard-shell helmet is made of polystyrene with a rigid cover. It gives good protection but you may need a sweat band as well.

Reflector belts help you to be seen in the dark or the rain.

Speedometers

A speedometer, or "computer", helps you to monitor your training progress. It fits on the handlebars and is wired to a sensor on the forks. Generally, the more expensive it is, the more functions it has.

As well as giving your speed and timing your ride, it might show your average speed, maximum speed and mileage, both this trip and since you first used it. Some also show your present and average cadence.

Buying a racing bike

If you want a new bike, you can either buy a complete model or buy a frame and choose components for it separately. (This is more expensive). Cheaper than both is to buy second-hand. A good compromise is to get a good second-hand frame and some new components.

Selecting a frame

A frame is measured by the length of the seat tube. As a rough guide, it should be about 25.5cm less than your inside leg measurement. Good frames are made of butted tubing throughout (see right), such as Reynolds 531 or Columbus SL.

Butted tubing is thinner in the central section and thicker at the joints for strength. It is rigid but light.

Buying a new bike

Even if you are buying a complete bike, the frame is the most important part to get right. You can improve on the components when you can afford to.

Handlebar stem

A frame is measured from the top of the seat tube to the center of the bottom bracket.

With about 8cm of seat post exposed, sit on the bike with your foot on the pedal in the downmost position. Your leg should be slightly bent.*

The width of the handlebars should be equal to your shoulder width.

With your elbow touching the point of the saddle, your fingertips should almost reach the handlebars. If they don't, you may need a longer or shorter handlebar stem.

Finding a good shop

You need to find a bike shop that specializes in lightweight racing bikes. A good shop will give you constructive advice and will help to fit you out with a bike that suits your needs, not just one that they want to sell. Ask other cyclists for recommendations and visit a few shops, looking out for the following:

★ A good range of frames and complete bikes plus a variety of components.
★ Helpful assistants who answer people's inquiries intelligently.
★ A workshop repair service and guarantee arrangements.

*See page 7 for more about saddle height.

Buying second-hand

A new bike loses up to a quarter of its value when first ridden, so buying second-hand can be good value. First, check the bike fits you (see previous page) and then check the following.

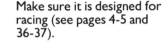

Make sure it is designed for racing (see pages 4-5 and 36-37).

Look for good quality tubing. To check that it is butted, flick it with your fingernail. The note should change as you move away from the joints.

If the bike has been in an accident, the frame might be bent or weakened. Check for dents behind the headset on the down tube and top tube.

Spin the wheels to see if they run straight, checking from the front and the side. Support your finger on a chainstay or fork and hold it against the rim as a guide.

Check for dents in the rims. Check that the spokes are taut. Saggy or bent spokes will need replacing.

Where to look

★ Bike shops which deal in used bikes or frames.
★ The classified pages in cycling magazines.
★ Your club noticeboard. Keen cyclists often change their bikes and equipment.
★ Advertisements in bike shop windows.

The pedals should be at right angles to the cranks.

Check that the teeth on the chainwheels and sprockets are not worn where they pull on the chain.

Worn tooth

The forks should be in line with the head tube. Look from the side to check. It helps to hold something straight like a ruler up against them.

Take someone more experienced along to check the bike before you hand over any money. If the bike needs new parts, estimate the total cost of the bike and the new parts. Compare this with the price of a new, similar bike to see if the asking price is a fair one.

Trying a bike out

Trying more than one bike is a useful comparison. Make sure you get the saddle and handlebars adjusted to fit you before you start.

★ Check that the brakes work smoothly and quickly.
★ Try the gears to make sure they change easily.
★ The bike should ride in a straight line if you take your hands off the bars.
★ Make sure the bike fits you and gives you a comfortable ride.

Looking after your bike

To get the best from your bike, you need to keep it clean and in good running order. At the bottom of the next page are some things you should check each time you set out to ensure that it is safe to ride.

Cleaning the bike

After a ride, wipe any water or sweat off the frame. Sweat is very corrosive.

The bike needs a thorough cleaning at least once a month. This lengthens the life of its components and gives you a chance to check for worn parts. If you use protective cream on your hands when cleaning the bike, it is easier to get the dirt and grease off them afterwards. Wear rubber gloves when using strong chemicals.

You will need:
A bucket of warm, soapy water
A soft brush
Rags for drying
An old toothbrush
Degreasing agent (or white spirit)
Light oil or spray lubricant
Rubber gloves and protective cream
Car wax polish
Chrome polish
An old paint tin or jam jar

Supporting the bike

It is easier to clean or make adjustments to the bike if it is supported on a repair stand. If you don't have one, you can improvise by hanging the frame from a clothes line.

Repair stand

Take the wheels out and use a stick to hold the chain in place as shown.

The stick goes through the holes in the seat stays.

Cleaning procedure

Wearing rubber gloves, use an old toothbrush to clean the sprockets, chainwheels, derailleur and brake mechanisms with some degreasing agent. (Pour some into a jam jar or paint tin.) Using a soft brush, wash the frame and wheels in soapy water, starting at the top and working down. Rinse all parts in clean water and dry them thoroughly with a rag.

Use a rag dampened with degreasing agent to clean the chain. Hold the rag over the chain and, with your other hand turn the cranks counterclockwise. Let the chain run through the rag for several turns. If the chain is very dirty, remove it with a chain tool as follows.

Put the chain in the end slot of the tool and line up the point with one of the rivets. Turn the tool lever clockwise until the point of the tool touches the rivet. Keep turning to drive the rivet just far enough to free the inner link. Don't push the rivet right out as this makes it very difficult to reconnect the chain. Soak the chain in some degreasing agent for a few hours. Hang it up to dry before replacing it.

Point of chain tool pushes rivet out of inner link.

Lubricating and polishing

After cleaning, you need to lubricate the bike with either light oil or spray lubricant. Wipe off any excess, especially from the outside of the chain, and keep it away from brake blocks and wheel rims.

Rub in some wax polish to protect the frame but be careful to keep it off the wheel rims. You can protect the rims and cranks with chrome polish but wear rubber gloves when using it.

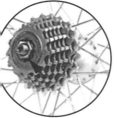

Tilt the rear wheel away from you. Run some oil into the freewheel mechanism and over the sprockets.

Lubricate the derailleur at the points where the mechanism pivots.

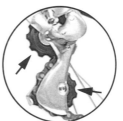

Lubricate the roller (jockey) wheels where they run on their axles.

Lubricate the front changer at the four points where it pivots, at the pivot bolts.

With the back wheel on, lubricate each chain link. Turn the pedals backward to move the chain.

Lubricate the gear cables wherever they emerge from the outer housing.

Lubricate the brake calipers at the pivot bolts and where they run against the springs.

Lubricate the brake cables wherever they emerge from the outer housing.

Before you ride

Check the following before a ride.

★ Examine the tires and remove any foreign bodies, such as grit or glass, with a pair of tweezers.

★ Repair any small cuts in the tires with fast-acting glue. You will need to let them down to do this.

★ If there is any movement when you pull the brake levers on fully and push forward, you need to adjust the brakes (see page 35).

★ Pump the tires up fully: the correct pressure should be printed on the tire wall. Use a tire pressure gauge to measure this, as shown in the picture.

★ Make sure that the quick-release levers are closed.

Pressure gauge fits over tire valve.

Dial shows tire pressure.

33

Basic maintenance

Parts wear out or work loose very gradually, so you should establish a routine for checking them regularly.

Brakes need checking weekly and the parts mentioned below at least every three months.

Crank bolts

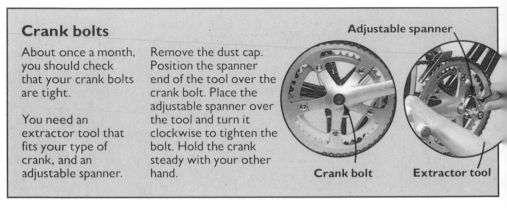

Adjustable spanner

About once a month, you should check that your crank bolts are tight.

You need an extractor tool that fits your type of crank, and an adjustable spanner.

Remove the dust cap. Position the spanner end of the tool over the crank bolt. Place the adjustable spanner over the tool and turn it clockwise to tighten the bolt. Hold the crank steady with your other hand.

Crank bolt

Extractor tool

Gears

To stop the chain jumping off the sprockets or chainwheels when you change into top or bottom gear, you need to adjust the derailleur or the front changer mechanisms.

Locate the high and low adjusting screws. These limit the range of movement of the derailleur or front changer. With a small screwdriver, adjust a screw half a turn at a time and check the gears again.

Adjusting screws on derailleur.

Adjusting screws on front changer.

Hub adjustment

Hubs, like other moving parts, contain bearings which need occasional adjustment. Correct adjustment means that the wheel turns freely and smoothly and there is no play when you hold the axle and wiggle the wheel from side to side. ·
   To adjust a front hub, take the wheel out of the frame. Use a cone spanner and an adjustable spanner for the job.

Hold the cone with the cone spanner as you loosen the locknut with the adjustable spanner. Remove the washer. Turn the cone an eighth to a quarter of a turn (clockwise to tighten, anticlockwise to loosen).* Hold the cone in place as you retighten the locknut. If the hub does not turn smoothly when adjusted, the hub bearings, cones or axle may need replacing (see page 36).

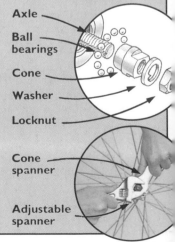

Axle

Ball bearings

Cone

Washer

Locknut

Cone spanner

Adjustable spanner

*It is important not to tighten or loosen the cones too much as this can damage the bearings.

Brakes

If there is more than 2in of movement at the brake levers between the off and on positions, loosen the locknut on the calipers. Then screw the adjuster counterclockwise. If it is as far as it will go, you need to tighten the cable as follows.

Screw the adjuster down (clockwise) and with a small spanner loosen the cable anchor bolt. Press the calipers together as you pull the cable down and retighten the bolt. You need more than two hands to do this, so ask someone to help.

Adjuster
Locknut
Brake cable
Cable anchor bolt

Check that each brake block strikes the wheel rim and not the tire itself.

At the same time, check the blocks for wear and replace both blocks even if only one is worn.

To adjust or replace a block, undo the acorn nut at the side of the calipers with a spanner. Apply the brake, hold the block in position and tighten the nut. Make sure the block is facing the right way. Most have an arrow and the word "forward" imprinted in the rubber.

Acorn nut
Brake block

The blocks should spring clear of the rims when you release the levers. If they stick or are slow to react, the calipers may be poorly lubricated, or you may need to adjust the pivot bolt as follows.

With a small spanner, loosen first the locknut (if there is one) and then the adjusting nut in front very slightly.*

Retighten the locknut and check the brakes again.

Adjusting nut
Locknut
Calipers

The brake levers should be firmly fixed to the bars. If they are loose, tighten the bolt inside the brake lever. You will need either a screwdriver or an allen key to do this.

First, loosen the cable anchor bolt to release the cable. Pull on the brake levers and pull the cable aside. You will then be able to get to the bolt to tighten it.

Cable
Bolt inside brake lever.
Brake lever

At the same time, check for fraying brake cables, especially at the cable anchor bolt and inside the brake lever.

Replace the cables if any strands are broken.

If your bike has concealed cables (aero levers), release the cable at the anchor bolt. Push the end of the cable up as far as the adjuster and pull on the brake lever. The cable will protrude from the lever.

Aero levers
Check for wear here.

---

*Be careful not to loosen the pivot bolt too much or the calipers will rock forward as you brake.

Maintaining bearings

The moving parts of a bike – the hubs*, bottom bracket, headset and pedals – all contain bearings. If the bearings are not properly adjusted they wear unevenly and damage the component. As well as checking the adjustment every so often, the ball bearings should be replaced and lubricated every three to six months.

Some bikes contain bearings in a sealed unit which does not need overhauling. Good ones may take up to ten years to wear out. Then you need to replace the whole unit.

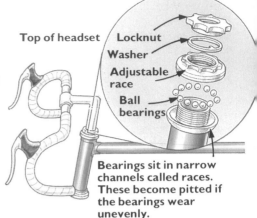

Top of headset — Locknut
Washer
Adjustable race
Ball bearings

Bearings sit in narrow channels called races. These become pitted if the bearings wear unevenly.

Annual overhauling

You should give your bike a thorough overhaul every year before the race season. This involves dismantling it completely so that you can clean, lubricate and replace parts if necessary.

There is not enough space in this book to describe how to do this but the list on the right gives you an idea of what needs to be done. Ask an experienced person to help you, or buy or borrow a good bike maintenance book.

★ Bottom bracket. Dismantle down to the spindle. Check for pitting and wear from contact with the bearings.
★ Gears. Replace the cables as they stretch and rust over time. Check the alignment of the gear mechanisms (see page 34).
★ Headset. Dismantle it to check the bearings (see top of page). Replace any damaged or corroded parts.
★ Brakes. Replace the brake cables. Run through all the checks on page 35.
★ Wheels and hubs. Check the hub bearings. Check the spokes for damage and replace if necessary. See that the spokes are tight and that the wheels run true (straight).
★ Chain and chainwheels. Replace the chain if you can lift it more than 1/8in off the chainwheels. Check for worn or bent chainwheel teeth.
★ Seatpin and handlebar stem. Remove these (see below) and grease them lightly to stop them from rusting into position.

Saddle and handlebar adjustments

To remove, raise or lower the saddle, loosen the seat bolt using either a spanner or an allen key. To move the saddle backward or forward, loosen nuts A and B. (On some bikes, you loosen the bolt under the top of the seat post.)

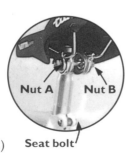

Nut A **Nut B**

Seat bolt

To remove, raise or lower the handlebars, loosen the expander bolt on top of the stem. Tap the top sharply to release the wedge inside. To change the angle of the bars, loosen bolt A. Tighten all bolts after adjustment.**

Expander bolt

Bolt A

*See page 34 for how to adjust hub bearings.
**You should check seat and handlebar bolts are tight every few weeks.

Club cycling

As a member of a cycling club, you are more likely to get a place in local or national races and build up your racing experience. The club coach can help you to choose races and set objectives. You can also pick up tactics and techniques from more experienced members.

Finding a club

A bike shop may be able to give you details of local cycling clubs. Otherwise, contact the national cycling federation (address on page 45). Try to find out how the local clubs differ. Here are some questions you may want to ask about them.

1. What sort of cycling are most members interested in? Don't join a touring club if you want to race.

2. Is the club affiliated with the national cycling federation and time trials council? This will enable you to enter national events.

3. Does the club coach organize any winter training such as weight and circuit training?

4. Does the club have a sponsor who gives some financial support? This might cover transportation to races and some equipment.

Chain gangs

Groups of riders, often from more than one club, may meet up and race against one another in mock competition. These are called chain gangs. If you get the chance, join one a little above your standard so that you are stretched but still able to keep up and take your turn at the front. Chain gangs tend to be hard rides rather than gentle runs and are therefore good race practice.

Entering races

Cycle races are usually promoted by local clubs or national federations. Entry forms should be sent in at least three weeks in advance to be sure of getting a place.* (Your club secretary will have a supply of standard forms.) For road races, you also need a race license which you buy from the cycling federation. It lasts for a year.

About a week before the race, you should receive course details and a list of competitors. These will help you to plan your race tactics. For a time trial, you will also receive a starting time.

On the day of the race, try to arrive about an hour before the start (a little less for time trials). You then need to report to the following people:

The **examiner** checks your bike and gives you an examination ticket if he is satisfied that it is in good working order.**

The **license steward** takes your examination ticket and race license and gives you a race number to wear.

The **chief commissaire** then calls all the riders together (either in the changing room or at the start line) to warn them of any dangers on the route or any changes that have had to be made due to hazards such as floods.

After the race, the **chief judge** will tell you how you placed in the race and whether you have scored any points.

Collect your race license from the license steward. The chief commissaire then makes a note in it of any points gained. This is called endorsing your license.

*You can normally enter club time trials and cyclo-cross races on the day.
**This only applies to road races and criteriums.

Design and technology

Basic bike design has changed little since the 1900s. However, the development of lightweight materials, such as aluminum alloys and carbon fiber has improved its efficiency. The bike on the opposite page shows some recent design innovations.

Frame geometry

As you pedal, you exert a force on one side of the bike and then the other. This makes the frame bend slightly, using up energy. Energy loss is reduced on a racing bike by making the frame stiffer.

Increasing the angles shown on the diagram and shortening the chainstays makes the frame shorter and therefore stiffer.

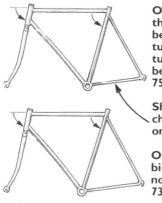

On a racing bike the angle between the seat tube and top tube is normally between 73° and 75°.

Shorter chainstays than on touring bike.

On a touring bike, the angle is normally 72° or 73°.

Forks

The steeper and straighter the forks, the more responsive the bike will be to small movements.

Increasing the angle marked at the top of the fork diagram makes them steeper. The amount the forks bend at the bottom is called the fork rake. On a racing bike, the fork rake is usually 2in or less.

Fork rake

Disc wheels

As the spokes go around on a normal wheel, they catch the air and slow you down. Disc wheels reduce this effect as the air flows smoothly over the disc's surface. However, bikes are often only fitted with a rear disc: a front disc makes the bike difficult to steer in a sidewind because air cannot pass through it.

The best discs are light carbon fiber and are very expensive. Plastic or fabric clip-on covers are a cheaper alternative.

The *Union Cycliste Internationale* (UCI) which sets the standards for all races does not allow aerodynamic attachments. Disc wheels are permitted as they are part of the bike. Clip-on wheel covers are illegal.

Index gears

On ordinary (open) gears, you judge the movement of the shift lever by feel or ear. With an index system, you move the lever until it clicks into a position that lines the derailleur up with the sprocket automatically. This is done by means of stops inside the lever mechanism.

Expensive index systems can be changed to the ordinary system by a switch on the side of the lever.

Aerodynamics

As you ride, your effort is going into overcoming friction. There is friction between the road and your wheels (called rolling resistance), between the moving parts of your bike, and between the air and your body and bike (called aerodynamic drag).

As you pick up speed, you fight aerodynamic drag more than anything else. Some things help to reduce this, such as a streamlined position, skin-tight clothing and certain design features such as disc wheels.

Handlebar extensions

Handlebar extensions, sometimes called aero bars, give you the option of a very streamlined position. They clamp on to your existing bars with allen key bolts.*

Oval chainwheels

Oval (elliptical) chainwheels have the effect of slightly changing gear as you pedal. This means that when your cranks are horizontal and your are able to push your hardest, your are in a larger gear. However, elliptical chainwheels can also interfere with the development of a smooth pedaling style.

Specialized bikes

Although standard racing bikes have not changed much, there have been some specialist developments which improve speed or performance in certain events.

Low profile bikes

Low profile bikes are generally used in time trials. The front wheel is smaller, the head tube short and the bars shaped upward and forward to give a very low riding position. In some cases, the seat tube is curved to allow the back wheel to come in closer. This is the ultimate racing bike for combating aerodynamic drag and improving speed.

The front wheel has fewer spokes than usual for lightness.

Mountain bikes

Mountain bikes were first designed for racing off-road and they are often seen in cyclo-cross races. Three chainwheels provide gears low enough for steep, broken ground. Because of the comfortable riding position, they are also popular with city riders.

Straight handlebars for a comfortable position.

Thick, knobby tires for rough ground.

Recumbent bikes

The rider pedals a recumbent bike from a low, reclined position. The aerodynamic drag is 20% less than on an upright bicycle. The UCI does not allow them in any of their races but enthusiasts organize their own races.

The recumbent position supports the rider so that the whole effort goes into pedaling.

Handlebar extensions are illegal in some races.

Safety on the bike

Although crashes and falls are not always avoidable, riding safely may help prevent them. Just like any other road user, you must be familiar with the rules of the road and consider other vehicles.

Traffic and other hazards

Although bikes have the same rights as other vehicles, as a cyclist you are more vulnerable. Make sure all your signals are clear and be definite and confident in your movements. The following points are relevant to bike riding in general, not specifically race training.

★ Many cities have marked cycle paths. Take advantage of these if there are any along your route.

★ Obey all traffic signs and signals. Be ready to stop at pedestrian crossings.

★ Check behind before pulling out to pass a parked vehicle. Remember that the driver may open the door in your path.

★ If you have to cross the path of vehicles behind in order to turn off the road, look back well in advance to check when it will be safe to move across. Signal clearly and check again before you maneuver.

★ Except in very slow traffic, leave at least three bicycle lengths between you and the vehicle ahead in case it stops suddenly or turns in front of you.

★ Exhaust fumes from heavy traffic are very unhealthy. Wearing a mask can help or better still, look for alternative back roads.

★ Ride far enough away from the edge of the road to avoid drains and gutters.

★ Colorful clothing and a reflector band enable drivers to see you from much further away than without them. Use reflectors and lights in dull weather as well as at night.

★ Keep your eyes on the road. To check behind, it is quicker and easier to duck your head down rather than twist it to the side.

★ You will find it easier to accelerate out of sticky situations if you are in a medium gear in which you can speed up without too much effort.

★ Before stopping, look behind and come to a halt slowly. Unless in an emergency, never surprise riders or drivers behind by skidding to a halt.

★ On country roads, give horses and other animals a very wide berth. It is better to keep pedaling as the clicking noise of the freewheel may frighten the animal.

★ Bear in mind that, early or late in the day, drivers may be blinded by a low sun and miss seeing you altogether.

The highway code

If you are unfamiliar with the highway code, it would be a good idea to buy or borrow a copy from your local library. It explains the rules of the road and the signs which you need to be able to recognize. All road users are supposed to know the highway code.

You may find a national cycling proficiency scheme useful even if you are quite an experienced cyclist. These train you to recognize and avoid risky situations and to cycle according to the highway code. The courses usually only last a couple of days and are free.

Crashes

In races and when you are training at high speeds, falls and collisions can happen so fast that there is little time to avoid them. The best you can do is to be alert and try to anticipate danger by keeping your eyes on the road ahead. Below are some situations in which you need to take special care.

Riding in a bunch

Leave at least 6in between your front wheel and the back wheel of the rider in front. If your wheels touch, you will be thrown violently over the handlebars.

The leaders of a bunch should warn of any danger in the road. They should point to an obstacle such as a pothole as they pass it and you should do the same to those behind you.

Bumpy roads

On bumpy roads, sit back on the saddle and hold the tops of the bars, with your elbows well bent. Look out for cracks or ridges in the road. If you hit one at speed, it can throw you sideways. If you spot it in time, try using the avoidance technique described on page 10.

Slippery surfaces

To avoid skidding on wet, oily or leaf-strewn surfaces, sit as upright as you can. Shift your weight back, don't rise off the saddle and avoid any sudden movements or hard braking.

Steep hills

It is easy to lose control of the steering when you are speeding downhill. Try to stay relaxed and in command by gripping the handlebars firmly and leaning into corners. Also, beware of loose gravel and leaves that gather at the bottom of hills. You can easily skid on these if you hit them at speed, especially if you are trying to corner at the same time.

Finishing a race

The elation of finishing a race makes it easy to lose concentration, especially if you are first over the line. Don't take your focus off the road ahead until you have come to a halt. Take care when turning round that you don't collide with other riders crossing the line.

Injuries

Deal with any injury as soon as possible. Cuts and scratches should be cleaned with warm water and some sort of antiseptic cream or lotion. Then cover the area to protect it from dust and dirt. Bruises can be treated with an ice pack (a bag of frozen peas is ideal).

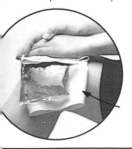

Press the ice pack gently against the bruised area for about 20 minutes.

Put a thin towel between the skin and the ice pack to avoid ice burn.

Falling off

Here are some ways in which you may be able to reduce the injury if you do fall.

★ Wear a good helmet.*
★ Relax your arms and legs to absorb the shock of a fall.
★ Wear gloves (track mitts) to save your hands from being scratched.

★ As you fall, curl up and try to go into a roll to absorb the shock. Tuck your head in and fold your arms around it.

*More about helmets on page 29.

Cycling injuries

At one time or another, you may be unlucky enough to suffer from cycling-induced injuries or conditions such as those listed below. Here are some suggestions for prevention and treatment.

Cramps

Cramps in a calf muscle are often the result of insufficient training or not warming up properly. Pre-race massage can help to prepare your muscles against cramps. After a ride, massage helps to free the muscles. If you get cramps on a ride, try pushing your heels down hard as you pedal or stop and relax the muscle.

To relieve cramps, try pressing hard into the thickest part of the muscle and hold for a count of ten. The pain should gradually ease.

Saddle sores

The chamois or synthetic padded insert in cycling shorts helps to prevent chaffing of the groin area as long as the insert is worn directly next to the skin. Wash your shorts after each wearing with a gentle soap powder that won't destroy the chamois.

You can buy chamois creams which you rub into the insert as added prevention to chaffing. If you get saddle sores, avoid using soap but bathe the area with warm water and a hypo-allergenic cleanser for sensitive skin. If possible, stop riding for a while to let the sores heal.

Numb hands or feet

If you suffer from numb hands, try shifting their position on the handlebars more often. Padded cycling gloves (track mitts) help as they absorb some vibration from the road. Numb feet may result from your toe straps being too tight. System pedals are more comfortable as they work without toe straps.

System pedals have quick-release bindings that grip the soles of your shoes very tightly. You don't need toeclips.

Knee and other joint problems

Pain in your knees, lower back or shoulders may be due to an incorrect position on the bike. The riding position should never fully extend the legs, arms or back. Knee problems can start if your foot is misaligned on the pedal. Try adjusting the cleats, or your shoeplates if you have system pedals.

After a ride

Even on a hot day, put on some extra clothing and warm down after a ride. As soon as you can, have a shower. This is relaxing and rejuvenating and helps to fend off stiffness.

When not to ride

A rise in body temperature or normal pulse rate* are indications that you are unwell and should not exert yourself. As you recover, revert to training at a low level and build up slowly.

*More about pulse rate on page 26.

Food and nutrition

Cycling demands a lot of energy from your body. The main energy source in food are carbohydrates but proteins, fats, vitamins and minerals are also essential nutrients. A healthy diet might include a variety of the foods in the chart below although the highest percentage should be in the form of carbohydrates.

Nutrients	Good sources	Uses in the body
Carbohydrates	Cereals, bread, rice, potatoes, pasta, peas, beans.	These are the primary fuel source. Brown or wholemeal varieties contain more fiber which helps the food pass through the digestive system.
Fats	Vegetable oils, margarine, peanut butter, full-fat milk, cheese, butter.	During prolonged exercise, fats can be used as energy fuel. An excess is stored as body fat. Vegetable fat is better for you than animal fat.
Proteins	Dairy products, meat, fish, peas, beans, nuts, seeds.	Proteins are essential for growth and the repair of damaged body tissue.
Vitamins and minerals	Fresh fruit and vegetables.	These are vital for the regulation of body processes.

Eating for the race

Your last big meal should be at least three hours before the race. Otherwise, you may suffer from dreadful stomach cramps during the race. This is because your digestive system may be starved of the energy it needs to digest the meal. Instead, the energy is being diverted to your muscles.

It is a good idea to make this last big meal dinner the night before the race. Try to eat plenty of carbohydrates as this will constitute your source of energy for the race.

Breakfast

On the morning of the race, have a moderately-sized, carbohydrate-based breakfast and a hot drink.

During the race

You can carry water on any race if you think you might want a drink. In races over 40km, you will certainly need one.*

Instead of water, you could take an energy drink. This tops up your fluid level when you are working energetically and sweating. It replaces lost glucose, salts and minerals and is easily absorbed.

In a race over 75km, you will also need food to replenish your energy supplies. Fruit muffins, fruit and protein bars are easily digested and satisfy your stomach.**

After the race

Finish the day off with a carbohydrate based meal and plenty of fluid. Eat plenty of protein the following day.

*Water flavored with fruit juice is ideal.
**More about race food on page 13.

Gear restrictions

In some races, there is a maximum gear restriction to prevent riders straining in too high a gear and damaging their muscles and joints. Because the same gear makes different-sized wheels travel different distances, the maximum gear is measured by the distance traveled per crank revolution.

You can get details about gear restrictions from your club or cycling federation. To check your own top gear, consult a table such as the one below or work it out as shown.

Using a gear table

Find the sprocket and chainwheel size of your highest gear on the table. Where the sprocket column meets the chainwheel row is the distance covered per crank revolution. This table is for standard sprint rims with normal road tubular tires and 700c* rims with racing tires.

Adjusting the gears

If your highest gear exceeds the gear restriction, you need to adjust the derailleur mechanism so that it does not move the chain on to the smallest sprocket. You can find out how to make this adjustment on page 34.

Gear table

CHAIN-WHEEL SIZE	SPROCKET SIZE														
	12	13	14	15	16	17	18	19	20	21	22	23	24	25	26
40	7·01	6·47	6·01	5·61	5·26	4·95	4·67	4·42	4·20	4·00	3·82	3·66	3·50	3·36	3·23
41	7·19	6·63	6·16	5·75	5·39	5·07	4·79	4·53	4·31	4·10	3·92	3·75	3·59	3·44	3·31
42	7·36	6·79	6·31	5·89	5·52	5·19	4·90	4·65	4·41	4·20	4·01	3·84	3·68	3·53	3·39
43	7·54	6·96	6·46	6·03	5·65	5·32	5·02	4·76	4·52	4·30	4·11	3·93	3·77	3·61	3·47
44	7·71	7·12	6·61	6·17	5·78	5·44	5·14	4·87	4·63	4·40	4·20	4·02	3·85	3·70	3·56
45	7·89	7·28	6·76	6·31	5·91	5·57	5·26	4·98	4·73	4·50	4·30	4·11	3·94	3·78	3·64
46	8·06	7·44	6·91	6·45	6·04	5·69	5·37	5·09	4·84	4·60	4·39	4·21	4·03	3·86	3·72
47	8·24	7·60	7·06	6·59	6·18	5·81	5·49	5·20	4·94	4·70	4·49	4·30	4·12	3·95	3·80
48	8·42	7·77	7·21	6·73	6·31	5·94	5·61	5·31	5·05	4·80	4·59	4·39	4·20	4·03	3·88
49	8·59	7·93	7·36	6·87	6·44	6·06	5·72	5·42	5·15	4·91	4·68	4·48	4·29	4·12	3·96
50	8·77	8·09	7·51	7·01	6·57	6·19	5·84	5·53	5·26	5·01	4·78	4·57	4·38	4·20	4·04
51	8·94	8·25	7·66	7·15	6·70	6·31	5·96	5·64	5·36	5·11	4·87	4·66	4·47	4·28	4·12
52	9·12	8·41	7·81	7·29	6·83	6·43	6·07	5·75	5·47	5·21	4·97	4·75	4·56	4·37	4·20
53	9·29	8·58	7·96	7·43	6·96	6·56	6·19	5·86	5·57	5·31	5·06	4·84	4·62	4·45	4·28
54	9·47	8·74	8·11	7·57	7·10	6·68	6·31	5·97	5·68	5·41	5·16	4·94	4·73	4·54	4·36
55	9·64	8·90	8·26	7·71	7·23	6·80	6·42	6·08	5·78	5·51	5·25	5·03	4·82	4·62	4·45
56	9·82	9·06	8·41	7·85	7·36	6·93	6·54	6·19	5·89	5·61	5·35	5·12	4·91	4·70	4·53

Measuring the distance

With the cranks vertical, mark the ground directly below. Move the bike back for one revolution of the crank and draw another mark. The distance between the marks is the distance traveled per crank revolution. Alternatively, you can work the distance out as follows.

Divide the number of chainwheel teeth by the sprocket teeth. Multiply by 3.142 (known as pi). Multiply by the diameter of the wheel. For example:

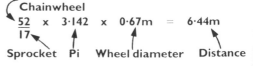

Chainwheel

$$\frac{52}{17} \times 3 \cdot 142 \times 0 \cdot 67m = 6 \cdot 44m$$

Sprocket Pi Wheel diameter Distance

*700c describes a standard-size racing or touring wheel.

Useful addresses

To find out more about cycling events or clubs in your area, you can contact your country's national cycling federation. You probably need to belong to the federation to enter certain races and some have facilities such as automatic insurance against bike accidents.

International

Union Cycliste Internationale (UCI)
6 Rue Amat
1202 Genève
Switzerland

Great Britain

British Cycling Federation
36 Rockingham Road
Kettering
Northamptonshire
NN16 8HG

Tel. 0536-412211

Road Time Trials Council
Dallacre House
Mill Road
Yarwell
Peterborough
PE8 6PS

Tel. 0780-782464

British Cyclo-Cross Association
59 Jordan Road
Sutton Coldfield
West Midlands
B75 5AE

Tel. 021-308-1246

Cycle Speedway Council
57 Rectory Lane
Poringland
Norwich
NR14 7SW

Tel. 05086-3880

British Triathlon Association
(Junior Team Manager)
4 Tynemouth Terrace
Tynemouth
NE30 4BH

Tel. 091-258-1438

USA

United States Cycling Federation
1750 East Boulder Street
Colorado Springs
CO 80909

Tel. 719-578-4581

Canada

Canadian Cycling Association
1600 Prom. James Naismith Dr.
Gloucester
Ontario
K1B 5N4

Tel. 613-748-5629

Australia

Australian Cycling Federation
68 Broadway
Sydney
NSW 2007

Tel. 02-281-8688

Australian Cycle Speedway Council
National Secretary
7 Broadford Crescent
Findon
South Australia 5023

Tel. 618 347 0655

New Zealand

New Zealand Amateur Cycling Association
PO Box 35-048
Christchurch

Tel. 03-851-422

Ireland

Federation of Irish Cycling
Halston Street
Dublin 7

Tel. 01-727524

Glossary

Aerobic activity An activity which relies on an energy system that uses oxygen to supply energy over a long period of time.

Aerodynamic drag The slowing down effect of the air on your body and bike as you ride.

Anaerobic activity An activity which relies on an energy system that uses stored muscle glycogen to give you a quick burst of energy.

Ankling A technique which increases pedaling power. You change the angle of your foot in order to pull up on the toeclips as well as push down on the pedals.

Attacking Making a calculated move to break away from a **bunch** in a race in order to gain a lead or split up the race.

Banking The ends of a cycle track which slope upwards to prevent the riders slipping as they speed round the bends.

Biathlon An event consisting of both cycling and running, sometimes called "run:bike:run" event.

Bit and bit A technique where riders in a group take turns to lead in order to share the effort and keep up the pace.

Break A rider or group of riders who pull away from a **bunch** in a race.

Bunch The main group of riders in a race.

Butted tubing Good-quality frame tubing which is thinner in the central section and thicker at the joints to make the frame rigid but light.

Cadence The rate at which your pedals go round measured in revolutions per minute (revs or rpm).

Chain-gang A group of riders from different clubs who meet for training runs.

Cleat A shoe plate that screws on to the sole of a cycling shoe and slots on to the edge of the pedal. It keeps the foot in position on the pedal.

Cone spanner A very thin spanner that fits the hub cones.

Criterium A type of **road race** that takes place on a closed circuit free from traffic, such as a park. Riders have to lap the circuit a set number of times.

Cycle speedway A fast and furious cycle sport that takes place on special shale tracks.

Cyclo-cross A winter sport that combines cycling with running and sometimes carrying the bike over obstacles and rough ground.

Disc wheel A type of wheel with flat surfaces instead of spokes, used to reduce the effects of **aerodynamic drag**.

Echelon A staggered line of riders. Riders position themselves slightly behind and either to the right or left of the rider in front in order to shelter from a sidewind.

Embrocation A type of oil used by cyclists. Applied lightly to the skin, it helps to keep the body warm.

Energy drink A preparation that you buy in powder form and mix with water. As a drink on long races or rides, it replaces lost glucose, salts and minerals as well as fluid.

Field Collective term for all the riders in a race.

Handicap race An event in which riders from different categories start at different times. This gives lower category riders a head start.

Handsling A technique used in a team **track race** to propel your partner into the race.

High-pressure tire A type of tire that has an inner tube, used on racing and touring bikes.

Hill climb A short grueling race against the clock up a very steep hill.

Honking Rising from the saddle to a standing position and using your body weight to increase the pressure on the pedals as you climb a steep hill.

Index gearing A gear system with a mechanism in the gear lever. As you move the lever, it clicks into position automatically.

Madison A team **track race** where the two riders in each team take turns to race for a certain distance.

Massed start event A **road race** in which all riders start together.

Oxygen debt A condition which can develop when you are riding hard. Your muscles start to burn or ache because your body cannot take in enough oxygen to remove toxic waste from anaerobic energy production.

Peloton The French word for **bunch**.

Pressure gauge A device that you can slot on to the tire valve which registers the air pressure in the tire.

Primes (pronounced preem) Interim targets to aim for during a **road race** where you can win extra points or prizes.

Pursuit A **track race** where two riders start at opposite sides of the track and try to catch each other up.

Randonnée A non-competitive ride over a varying distance (from 50km up to 1000km).

Reliability ride See **randonnée**.

Road race A race held on the open road. Distances vary from 40km to over 100km. There are no road races for juveniles.

Rolling resistance The friction between your bike tires and the road surface as you ride.

Scratch race A massed start road race where all categories ride the same distance.

Skinsuit An all-in-one garment usually made of lycra. These are often worn in track or short-distance events where pockets are not needed for carrying food.

Slipstreaming Riding directly behind another rider in order to travel as fast but with less effort.

Speedometer A small gadget sometimes called a bike computer, that fits on to the handlebars. It has a sensor attached to the forks and might show **cadence** as well as mileage and speed.

Stage race A long road race such as the *Tour de France* or the British Milk Race. Each day (or stage) is a separate race with its own prizes. At the end, each rider's time for all stages are totaled. The shortest overall time wins.

System pedals An alternative to normal pedals and toeclips. Shoe-plates fitted to the soles of cycling shoes slot into the pedals which have quick-release bindings.

Time trial A race on the road where riders start at one-minute intervals and race against the clock.

Track mitts Padded cycling gloves, (often fingerless).

Track race Any event that takes place on a cycle track such as a sprint, **pursuit** or **madison**.

Triathlon An event that combines running, cycling and swimming in continuous sequence.

Tubular tire (tub) Tubeless tire used on a sprint rim. It is either cemented to the rim or fixed with double-sided tape.

Tire pressure The amount of air pressure in a tire. It is measured in pounds per square inch (psi) or atmospheres (bars). The recommended amount of air for a tire is printed on the side of the tire, in bars or psi.

Wheel-following See **slipstreaming**.

Index

With thanks to: Robin Kyte and Fred Williams Cycles Ltd, Wolverhampton.